A Note to Parents and Teachers

Kids can imagine, kids can laugh and kids can learn to read with this exciting new series of first readers. Each book in the Kids Can Read series has been especially written, illustrated and designed for beginning readers. Humorous, easy-to-read stories, appealing characters, and engaging illustrations make for books that kids will want to read over and over again.

To make selecting a book easy for kids, parents and teachers, the Kids Can Read series offers three levels based on different reading abilities:

Level 1: Kids Can Start to Read

Short stories, simple sentences, easy vocabulary, lots of repetition and visual clues for kids just beginning to read.

Level 2: Kids Can Read with Help

Longer stories, varied sentences, increased vocabulary, some repetition and visual clues for kids who have some reading skills, but may need a little help.

Level 3: Kids Can Read Alone

Longer, more complex stories and sentences, more challenging vocabulary, language play, minimal repetition and visual clues for kids who are reading by themselves.

With the Kids Can Read series, kids can enter a new and exciting world of reading!

POSTAL WORKERS

With thanks to Deby Martin at Canada Post — P.B. and K.L.

Acknowledgments
Thanks to Chris Bartsch, Canada Post, and Maureen Skinner Weiner for their review of the revised text.

 TM Kids Can Read is a trademark of Kids Can Press Ltd.

Kids Can Press acknowledges the financial support of the Government of Ontario, through the Ontario Media Development Corporation's Ontario Book Initiative; the Ontario Arts Council; the Canada Council for the Arts; and the Government of Canada, through the BPIDP, for our publishing activity.

Published in Canada by	Published in the U.S. by
Kids Can Press Ltd.	Kids Can Press Ltd.
29 Birch Avenue	2250 Military Road
Toronto, ON M4V 1E2	Tonawanda, NY 14150

www.kidscanpress.com

Edited by David MacDonald
Designed by Kathleen Collett
Educational consultant: Maureen Skinner Weiner, United Synagogue Day School, Willowdale, Ontario
Canadian reviewer: Chris Bartsch, Canada Post
Printed and bound in China

The hardcover edition of this book is smyth sewn casebound.
The paperback edition of this book is limp sewn with a drawn-on cover.

CM 05 0 9 8 7 6 5 4 3 2 1
CM PA 05 0 9 8 7 6 5 4 3 2 1

National Library of Canada Cataloguing in Publication Data
Bourgeois, Paulette
    Postal workers / written by Paulette Bourgeois ; illustrated by Kim LaFave.

(Kids can read)
ISBN 1-55337-746-X (bound).   ISBN 1-55337-747-8 (pbk.)

1. Postal service — Juvenile literature. 2. Postal service — Employees — Juvenile literature. I. LaFave, Kim II. Title. III. Series: Kids Can read (Toronto, Ont.)

HE6241.B68 2005   j383.4   C2004-901931-7

Kids Can Press is a *Corus* TM Entertainment company

POSTAL WORKERS

Paulette Bourgeois • Kim LaFave

Kids Can Press

"Oh, no!" says Gordon. "Grandma's birthday is only four days away and I haven't sent a card."

Gordon makes her a birthday card and puts it in an envelope.

He crosses his fingers. "I hope she gets this in time."

The card must travel all the way from Canada to the United States.

Gordon writes Grandma's address and
his address on the front of the envelope.
Then he walks to the post office to buy
a stamp.

The money for the stamp pays for the mail to travel from one place to another.

Gordon chooses a special stamp because Grandma likes to collect them. Then he buys a stamp for his own collection. He sticks Grandma's stamp onto the envelope and slides it into the mailbox.

Letters and small packages are dropped into local mailboxes. Every day, sometimes two or three times a day, a driver comes to collect the mail. The driver takes the mail to a place where the mail is sorted. Mail that is going to the same place is put together.

Most sorting is done by machine. Postal workers sort out special mail, parcels and letters that are too big or too small for the machines.

The mail goes through a machine that does three jobs in one. Just in case the human sorters missed an odd-sized envelope, the machine spits out all the mail that won't fit. Then it makes sure that all the fronts of the envelopes are facing the same direction.

Next, the machine cancels the stamps by making a mark on them. A stamp with this mark cannot be used again.

CANADA

UNITED STATES

Every address in Canada has a postal code made up of three letters from the alphabet and three numbers.

In the United States, every address has a zip code made up of five numbers. Most zip codes also have another code of four numbers added on.

Postal workers can tell almost exactly where you live. All they have to do is read your postal code or zip code!

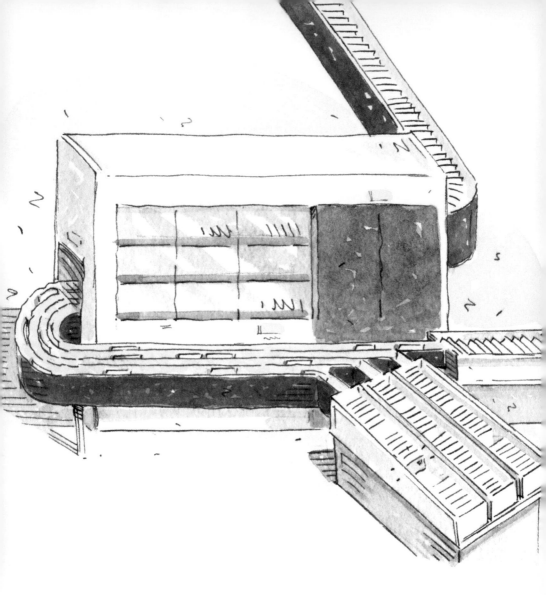

A machine reads the postal code or
zip code written on an envelope. Then the
machine writes the code on the envelope in
a computer language that looks like bars or
dots and bars.

Letters whiz through a sorting machine that reads the computerized postal codes. This machine sorts the envelopes onto different conveyor belts. Gordon's letter moves along the belt until it drops into a bag going to Grandma's city. The mail bags travel mostly by truck and by plane.

The card from Gordon goes to the postal station near his Grandma's house.

It is still cold, dark and early when Grandma's letter carrier gets to work. A postal worker has already sorted the mail into routes and put it into big, heavy bags.

The carrier sorts her mail into slots that are marked by street and building numbers. "Whew!" she says. "Must be a lot of birthdays coming up."

There's too much mail for the letter carrier to take all at once. She puts as much mail as she can carry into her satchel. A driver will take the rest of her mail to locked boxes, called relay boxes, on her route.

Letter carriers have to be ready for snow, sleet, sun or rain.

Their full bags can weigh up to 16 kg (35 lb.) each.

They need new shoes or boots every couple of months.

SUMMER

SPRING

Their uniforms have shoulder flashes on each arm.

They must be physically fit.

WINTER

AUTUMN

The letter carrier walks fast on her route. She steps around garbage cans, marches up steps and slides the mail into mail slots. She watches out for ice in the winter. And she hopes owners of angry dogs will keep them leashed and out of her way.

21

Letter carriers do not read the mail — not even funny postcards. But they do care who collects their mail and who doesn't. They know the elderly people on their route.

If their mail is not collected, the postal worker calls a special phone number to report it. Perhaps the person fell and can't get up. A relative or friend is sent to check. Postal workers save lives this way.

By the time the letter carrier reaches her relay box, her satchel is empty. She uses a key to open the lock and fills her satchel again. "What a beautiful yellow envelope," she says.

Grandma smiles when she opens her mailbox. "Goodness, something from Gordon! His card is early. My birthday isn't until tomorrow."

Grandma tapes Gordon's card on her fridge. She loves the card but she loves the stamp on the envelope, too. She adds Gordon's birthday stamp to her collection.

She already knows what she will send Gordon for his birthday — a card made of special paper with a dozen stamps from a dozen countries tucked inside an envelope.

Grandma addresses her envelope carefully
and seals it.

She puts the stamp here.

She puts her address on the top left corner
of the envelope like this:

> MRS A STRUTHERS
> 45 URBAN WAY
> PORTLAND OR   97208

She puts Gordon's address in the middle
of the envelope like this:

> Gordon Norman
> 2 Gulls Way
> Go By Chance NL A0B 2C3

Gordon checks his community mailbox
every day. Soon it will be his birthday.
Grandma always sends him a big envelope
with something special tucked inside.